P9-DGW-416

SKATE PARK Challenge

BY JAKE MADDOX

illustrated by Sean Tiffany

text by Anastasia Suen

Librarian Reviewer
Chris Kreie
Media Specialist, Eden Prairie Schools, MN
M.S. in Information Media, St. Cloud State University, MN

Reading Consultant
Mary Evenson
Middle School Teacher, Edina Public Schools, MN
M.A. in Education, University of Minnesota

STONE ARCH BOOKS
Minneapolis   San Diego

Impact Books are published by Stone Arch Books,
151 Good Counsel Drive, P.O. Box 669,
Mankato, Minnesota 56002.
www.stonearchbooks.com

Library of Congress Cataloging-in-Publication Data
Maddox, Jake.
　　Skate Park Challenge / by Jake Maddox; illustrated by Sean Tiffany.
　　p. cm. — (Impact Books. A Jake Maddox Sports Story)
　　Summary: Despite sabotage that put him in a wrist brace for
two weeks, Nick is determined to win an upcoming skateboarding
competition.
　　ISBN-13: 978-1-59889-064-8 (hardcover)
　　ISBN-10: 1-59889-064-6 (hardcover)
　　ISBN-13: 978-1-59889-241-3 (paperback)
　　ISBN-10: 1-59889-241-X (paperback)
　　[1. Skateboarding—Fiction. 2. Sports injuries—Fiction.] I. Tiffany,
Sean, ill. II. Title. III. Series: Maddox, Jake. Impact Books (Stone Arch
Books) Jake Maddox Sports Story.
PZ7.S94343Ska 2007
[Fic]—dc22　　　　　　　　　　　　　　　　　　　2006006078

Art Director: Heather Kindseth
Cover Graphic Designer: Heather Kindseth
Interior Graphic Designer: Kay Fraser

1 2 3 4 5 6 11 10 09 08 07 06

Chapter 1

School's Out

School was finally out for the year, and Nick could ride his skateboard all day. First thing every morning, Nick headed to the skate park. It was inside the city park, next to the swings.

One morning when Nick rode up to the park, he saw his best friend, Josh, standing at the park entrance.

"Hey, Josh," said Nick. He bent his knees and slammed his back foot down on the tail of his skateboard. Nick jumped up with the skateboard as it popped up into the air. After he landed, Nick rolled up to Josh.

"Nice ollie," said Josh. "Look at this." Josh pointed to a poster on a wooden post.

"'Bikes, Boards, and Blades Jam,'" read Nick. "It should say 'Boards, Bikes, and Blades.' Everyone knows skateboards are the best!"

"Keep reading," said Josh.

Nick looked at the poster again. "The pros are coming here," said Nick, "and they're going to have a competition for amateurs!"

"Well, not here exactly," said Josh. He pointed at the poster. "See. They'll be at the big park downtown."

"I can't afford that place," said Nick.

"Who can?" said Josh. "How can any grom afford that stuff?" Groms were boarders under the age of fourteen.

"But we can still win," said Nick. "I can see it now. I'm standing on the stage holding the first place trophy."

"Oh, no," said Josh. "You get second place. I'll win first place this year."

"Oh, yeah?" said Nick.

"Yeah," said Josh.

"We'll see about that," said Nick, and he skated into the park.

"Wait for me," said Josh.

Nick skated up one side of the half-pipe. "I wonder what the course will look like."

"Like this park," said Josh, "only bigger."

"I hope so," said Nick. He balanced his board at the top of the half-pipe. "This skate park is too small."

"It's getting more crowded by the minute," said Josh. "Look who's here."

Nick skated down the other side of the half-pipe. "I see him."

Nick watched as another kid entered the park. It was a boy from his school, Brandon.

Brandon rode his skateboard over to the swings and sat down.

He picked up some gravel from under the swings and started tossing it.

"Aren't you punks done, yet?" said Brandon with a sneer.

"We just started," said Josh.

"It's my turn," said Brandon, tossing more pebbles.

"There's plenty of room on the other side of the park," said Nick.

"I want to use the half-pipe here," said Brandon. "You punks can go practice over there."

Nick rode up the half-pipe and balanced his board on the lip at the top.

Then he pushed off and rode his board down the other side

"Forget it," said Nick. "I'm using it now."

"Yeah?" Brandon threw a fistful of gravel at Nick's board.

The skateboard wheels skidded over the gravel. The skateboard swerved out of control.

The nose tipped down and scraped against the wall of the half-pipe.

The skateboard wasn't moving, but Nick was.

He flew over his board and landed with a thud on the concrete.

Chapter 2

The Doctor's Office

Nick sat in the waiting room at the doctor's office. His right wrist was swollen to twice its normal size.

"Here we go again," said Mom.

"It wasn't my fault," said Nick. "Brandon threw gravel at my board."

"I know it wasn't your fault," Mom said, "but why do you always have to get in trouble with that Brandon boy?" His mom sighed.

Nick thought about his skateboard. The front of the board had hit the concrete and shattered.

"I'm fine," said Nick. "It looks worse than it really is. We don't have to stay."

"We're here," said Mom. "Let the doctor look at it."

"Okay, okay," said Nick.

The door to the waiting room opened. "Nick Jackson," said the nurse. Nick and his mom stood up.

"This way," said the nurse. He took Nick and Mom to waiting room three.

"Sit here," said the nurse. Nick climbed up onto the crinkly paper.

"How did this happen?" said the nurse as he looked closely at Nick's swollen wrist.

"Skateboarding," said Nick.

"I should have guessed," said the nurse. He wrote something on the papers in Nick's chart. "The doctor will be right with you," he said.

Knock, knock.

Doctor Sam Byers opened the door and came into the room.

"Hi, Doctor Byers," said Mom.

"Hello, Amanda," said Dr. Byers, "and Nick." Then he looked at Nick's arm. "What have we here?" he said.

"It's nothing," said Nick.

Dr. Byers pressed his fingers into Nick's wrist. Nick winced.

"I see," said Dr. Byers. "We'll have to do an X-ray to make sure you didn't break your wrist."

"Break my wrist!" said Nick. "It was just a fall."

"That's exactly how bones break," said Dr. Byers.

"Great," said Nick, "just great."

"Or it might be just a sprain like last time," said Dr. Byers.

"That's it," said Nick. "It's just a sprain. Now can I go?"

"Not so fast," said Dr. Byers. "We need to be sure it's not broken. I'll be right back," he said.

Great, Nick thought. My wrist will be broken just like my stupid skateboard. And it's all that Brandon's fault!

Chapter 3

Grounded!

Josh was waiting on the porch when Nick got back from the doctor's office.

"Well?" said Josh when Nick and his mom got out of the car.

"It's not broken," said Nick.

"Cool," said Josh.

"But I have to wear this stupid brace," said Nick.

"Not cool," said Josh.

Mom opened the door. "Why don't you come in, Josh," she said. "You two can do your skateboarding on the TV."

Nick and Josh walked over to the TV. "I have to wear wrist guards," said Nick.

"The pros wear them," said Josh.

"But I like to do things old school," said Nick. He reached over to pick up the video game controller, but his thumb wouldn't move.

"Man!" said Nick.

"What?" said Josh.

"I can't move my thumb!" said Nick. "It's too swollen."

"That stinks," said Josh. Mom came out of the kitchen with a bag of ice wrapped in a towel.

"Put this on your wrist," she said, "and keep your wrist above your heart."

"Above my heart?" said Nick.

"Sit here and put your arm up on the arm rest," she said.

"Okay, okay," said Nick. He took the ice and the towel. Then he sat on the couch and put his arm on the arm rest.

"Brandon stinks," said Nick.

"You should have heard what he said when you left the park," said Josh.

Nick frowned. "What did he say?"

"Brandon thinks he can win now that you're out of the way," said Josh.

"Out of the way?" said Nick. "He's the one that caused this! Thanks to Brandon I can't even ride a virtual skateboard."

Chapter 4

Lightning Board

Early the next morning, Nick's doorbell rang. He opened the door. "Hey, Josh," he said. "Come on in."

"How's your wrist today?" asked Josh as he walked in the door.

"Okay," said Nick.

"Great!" said Josh. "Let's go to the park."

"I can't," said Nick.

"Why not?"

"I'm grounded," said Nick.

"Grounded?"

"Mom won't let me go to the park," said Nick. "Besides, I can't practice without a board. And it's lame for me to take turns on your board. I need my own."

Josh opened the front door. He reached around and pulled a skateboard into the house. "You mean like this one?" he asked.

"Cool board!" said Nick.

The board was as long as his old one. It was painted silver. A lightning bolt ran down the middle, and the word "zero" was painted near the tail.

"What's 'zero'?" asked Nick.

"That's my brother's nickname," said Josh.

"This is your brother's board? Cool! He did some pretty sweet jumps with this board," said Nick.

Josh smiled. "Yeah, he did. Including the one that broke his leg. Look at the wheels," said Josh.

Nick turned the skateboard upside down. Two of the wheels looked smashed, and one of the axles was crooked.

"I can't ride this," said Nick.

"Your board's broken," said Josh. "But your wheels are good. My brother's wheels are totaled, but the board is still tight."

"We can do a switch!" said Nick.

"I knew you were smart," said Josh.

"A few minutes with a screwdriver and a wrench, and you'll be rolling at the park again," said Josh with a grin.

Nick shook his head. "I can't. No skateboarding for two weeks."

"Two weeks!" said Josh. "That's like, forever!"

"I know," said Nick. "But if I stay off my board, Mom will let me see the pros and I can compete with all the groms."

"Oh," said Josh.

"She'll even pay for it," said Nick.

"Wow! She usually makes **you** pay," said Josh.

"I know," said Nick. "So I agreed. No skateboarding for two weeks."

"But you can't let Brandon win," said Josh.

"Don't worry," said Nick. "He won't."

"But you have to keep practicing or you lose it," said Josh.

"Lose what?" said Nick.

"Your skill," said Josh.

Nick looked at his wrist. "But I promised," he said. "My mom will kill me if she finds out I've been riding my board."

"How will she know? She's at work," said Josh.

"But Mrs. Hannigan next door isn't," said Nick, "and she watches everything."

Nick frowned. There was no way he could practice at the park. And Josh was right. If he didn't practice, he might lose his skill. Maybe Brandon was going to win after all.

Chapter 5

Slow Motion

Clapping and whistling filled the hallway.

"What's that noise?" asked Josh.

"I was watching my skateboarding DVDs," said Nick. "I left the TV on."

"DVDs?" said Josh. He walked into the living room.

Nick followed him. "I always watch them before a competition," he said.

Josh pointed at the TV. "That was so smooth."

"See how he flipped the board?" said Nick. "Then he landed on it!"

"Awesome," said Josh.

"You can learn a lot from watching the pros," said Nick.

"Play that again," said Josh, and he sat down on his board in front of the TV.

"Wait until you see it in slow motion," said Nick. He hit the track button.

"I'm ready," said Josh.

Nick pressed the button. "First he does an ollie," said Nick. "Then he grabs the board with his left hand."

"Okay," said Josh.

"And the front of the skateboard comes up," said Nick, "so he reaches over."

"Yeah," said Josh.

"And he grabs the board with his left hand," said Nick.

"Okay," said Josh.

"He flips the board over," said Nick. "Now watch what happens."

"He lands on it," said Josh.

"And that's how you do an ollie fingerflip." Nick stopped the DVD.

"It doesn't look hard when you play it slow like that," said Josh, "but it's not so easy in real life."

"In real life it happens a lot faster," said Nick.

"Why does he grab it with his left hand?" asked Josh.

"I don't know," said Nick. "Hey, wait a minute! I didn't sprain my left hand, I sprained my right hand."

"So?" said Josh.

"So I can do this trick," said Nick.

"But what about your mom?" asked Josh. "And the lady next door?"

"I don't have to go outside to flip my skateboard over," said Nick. He reached down and flipped his board with his left hand.

"See?" said Nick. "I can do it with my left hand."

"But you have to jump and land with this trick too," said Josh. "Can you do that with a swollen wrist?"

"I already know how to do an ollie," said Nick. "I don't have to practice that."

"Everyone knows how to do an ollie," said Josh.

"But an ollie fingerflip," said Nick, "that's another story."

"I've never seen any of the kids at the skate park try it," said Josh.

"It's an old-school move," said Nick.

"You like old school," said Josh.

"Judges like old school, too," said Nick.

"They do if you can pull it off," said Josh.

"I can try," said Nick. "And trying is the only thing I can do right now."

Chapter 6

The Big Day

Two weeks dragged by, and finally the big day arrived. Nick went into the kitchen to eat breakfast.

"Up so early?" Mom asked.

"Today's the day," said Nick. "I have to get ready."

Mom smiled. "I know," she said. She opened a drawer. "I think you'll need these." She put a small paper bag on the table next to Nick.

"What's this?" said Nick.

"Look inside," said Mom.

Nick put his hand inside the paper bag and pulled out a plastic bag.

"Wrist guards," said Nick. "But Mom, I stayed off my skateboard for two weeks. Isn't that enough?"

"You promised Dr. Byers you'd wear them," said Mom.

"But I wore that stupid brace everyday," said Nick.

"The brace can't protect your other wrist," said Mom.

"I'll be fine," said Nick.

"I know, because the wrist guards will protect your wrists," said Mom. "And then we won't have to see Dr. Byers so often," she added.

"Okay, okay," said Nick. "I'll wear them. When can we leave?"

Mom looked at her watch. "I can be ready in ten minutes," she said. "How about you?"

"Ten minutes it is," said Nick. He took out a bowl and poured cereal into it.

After he finished eating, Nick put the bowl and spoon in the sink. Then he ran upstairs to get his board and helmet.

"Don't forget your wrist guards," said Mom. "They're still on the table."

"I won't," said Nick. He put on his knee pads and elbow pads. Then he came downstairs with his skateboard and his helmet.

"The wrist guards," Mom said again.

Nick picked up the package and tore it open. Then he stuffed the wrist guards in his back pocket.

"They won't do you any good back there," said Mom."

"Okay, okay," said Nick. "I'll put them on." Nick took the wrist guards out of his pocket and put them on. "Now can we go?"

Chapter 7

Sign In

I've been waiting for this for so long, thought Nick. They walked into the park and looked for the registration booth.

"I see it," said Nick. "It's over there by the band stand."

Nick and Mom walked across the park. Kids with bikes, skates, and skateboards were everywhere.

"Wow! The whole town must be here," said Nick.

"The whole county is more like it," said Mom.

There was a long line at the registration booth. Finally, they reached the front of the line.

"Sign here and here," said the lady at the booth. She handed Nick's mom a pen and some papers.

Then she looked at Nick. "I see you have all of your safety gear."

"You better believe it," said Mom as she signed the papers.

"We require it now," said the lady.

"I'm glad to hear it," said Mom. She looked at Nick. Nick sighed.

"So when are you competing?" asked Mom as they moved out of the line.

Nick looked at the schedule behind the booth. "Two o'clock," said Nick.

"Good," said Mom. "One of the girls called in sick, so I have to cover her shift today at the restaurant."

"Mom!" said Nick

"I'll be back by two," she said. "I told them I could only work part of her shift."

Chapter 8

"Hey, dude! Where's your mom going?" asked Josh.

Nick turned around. "Oh, hey. Didn't know you were there," he said. "She's going to work."

"Really?" said Josh.

"She'll be back for the competition," said Nick.

"I see you're wearing wrist guards," said Josh.

Nick nodded. "I hope I can ride my board with them on. They feel funny."

"You'll get used to them," said Josh. "It just takes a few days."

"Yeah, but I don't have a few days," said Nick.

"Have you seen Brandon yet?" asked Josh.

"There he is," said Nick.

Brandon rode his skateboard up to Josh and Nick.

"So, you're still alive," said Brandon. "Too bad."

"Knock it off, Brandon!" said Josh.

Brandon ignored him and kept staring at Nick. "I haven't seen you out in a while."

"Yeah, and we both know why," said Nick. "You tried to knock me out of the competition."

"I did what?" said Brandon.

"You know," said Nick. "The gravel you threw at my board."

"You're crazy," said Brandon.

"We saw you throw it," said Josh.

"Whatever," said Brandon. He looked away. "Hey, Victor, wait up!" Brandon rode his skateboard over to an older boy.

"Brandon thinks he can take Victor's place in the grom competition," said Josh.

"Brandon is all hot air," said Nick.

"I know," said Josh. "But now that Victor has a sponsor, he can't be top grom anymore. Someone else will be!"

"That's right," said Nick. "It will be you or me."

"Yeah!" said Josh.

"Let's go watch the pros," said Nick. "We can see some new tricks to copy."

"But they're not moving in slow motion," said Josh.

"No problem," said Nick. "No one expects us to be exactly like the pros anyway."

"Yeah," said Josh.

"But that won't stop me from copying the pros," said Nick.

"Me neither," said Josh.

"Hey, I'm still working on the ollie fingerflip," said Nick.

"How is that going?" asked Josh.

"Okay, I guess," said Nick.

"I can't do it yet," said Josh. "The board keeps landing on its side."

"I haven't done it with these wrist guards," said Nick, "so we'll have to wait and see."

Chapter 9

The First Run

"Skateboarders! We're ready to start," said the official.

Finally! thought Nick.

"Each skateboarder will have two runs on the course," said the official. "The grom with the best score from the two runs will be the winner."

The crowd cheered.

And that will be me, thought Nick.

I can't let Brandon beat me, not after what he did, Nick said to himself.

One by one, the littlest boarders, the grommets, had their turn on the course.

"I wish they'd hurry up and let us have a turn," said Nick.

"They always do the little kids first," said Josh. "They're almost done."

"I know, I know," said Nick. "Wait.They just called your name!"

"Wish me luck," said Josh.

"Luck," said Nick. He gave Josh a high five.

Josh stood up and rode his skateboard over to the start.

Then he rode onto the course and started by riding down the rail.

Josh rode the rails and the ledges. He rode up and down the half-pipe, too. Then the timer buzzed and Josh's time was up. He rode off the course with a smile on his face.

"Man, that is such a great course!" said Josh.

"I wish we had a big half-pipe like that at our park," said Nick. Then the official called Nick.

Nick rode his board over to the starting point. The timer started as Nick rode out onto the course. Nick popped his board up, then rode down the ledge.

The half-pipe was next. Nick rode up one side of the half-pipe and grabbed his board.

Nick landed on the lip at the top and turned around.

Then he rode down the half-pipe and up the other side. He grabbed his board in midair and landed at the top of the pipe.

Nick rode down the half-pipe and over to the rail. He popped his board up and rode down the rail backward.

Nick rode his board over to the half-pipe and flew up one side. He grabbed the front of his board as he went up. After he landed, Nick turned around again and rode back down.

Time for a new trick, Nick thought. A cannonball. He grabbed his board and crouched down low.

The judges should like that, he thought.

I'll finish up with a street trick. Nick rode over to the rail and popped up on it.

He rode down the rail with half the board in the air. As he reached the bottom, Nick wobbled and fell off.

The timer buzzed.

My time is up, and the last thing the judges saw was a mistake! thought Nick.

Well, at least the tricks were harder than the ones the little grommets did. That has to count.

Nick rode off to talk with Josh.

"Bad break," said Josh.

"It's okay," said Nick.

"It was a hard trick," said Josh. "It counts more than an easy one, even if you fall."

"Yeah," said Nick.

Brandon was next. He did a few tricks on the rail and the ledge and then moved over to the half-pipe.

"Nothing great," said Nick when Brandon was done.

"Only safe moves," said Josh.

But after all of the groms had their turns, Brandon was number one on the scoreboard. Josh was fourth and Nick was seventh.

"Seventh!" said Nick. "How can I be seventh?"

"You fell," said Josh.

"But it was a hard trick," said Nick. "Brandon didn't do any hard tricks."

"He didn't fall," said Josh. "Maybe that counts more this year."

"It shouldn't," said Nick. "Taking a chance should count more!"

Chapter 10

Final Scores

Nick looked over and saw someone giving Brandon a high five.

Brandon turned to look at Nick and flashed him a big, fake smile.

He really thinks he's going to win, thought Nick.

Nick looked at his wrist guards. Well, at least they haven't really bothered me the way I thought they would.

If I am going to crash and burn, thought Nick, I'm going to go out in style.

Nick waited for all the little groms to finish their second run. Then finally it was Josh's turn.

Josh did his second run and he was really smooth. The judges will like that, thought Nick.

Nick slapped Josh a high five when he came off the course.

Now it was Nick's turn. Nick rode over to the official.

"Can you wait until I get up on the half-pipe?" said Nick. "Then start the clock."

The official looked at Nick.

He knows that's the way the pros do it, thought Nick.

"Uh, okay," said the official.

Nick rode up to the top of the half-pipe and looked down.

Time for some fun!

Nick pushed off.

Down the half-pipe he rode, picking up speed.

As Nick rode back up the other side, he grabbed the middle of his board.

Then up to the top. Nick balanced his board on the edge of the half-pipe and waited three seconds. Axle stall!

Nick tipped his board and rode back down into the half-pipe.

As he came up the other side, Nick reached forward and grabbed the front of his board. Nose grab!

Then he rode up to the top of the pipe again.

Nick balanced his board on the edge. Then he twisted his body and pivoted the board around.

Back into the half-pipe he rode.

As he came up the other side, Nick crouched low and grabbed his board. Cannonball!

Nick came up the other side, and this time he pushed just the front wheel over the lip.

Then he rocked back and rolled down into the pipe. Rock and roll!

He rode back up the pipe, and both wheels went over the lip.

Then Nick popped the board and twisted his body around as he came down. Blunt to fakie!

My time is almost up! It's now or never, Nick thought.

As Nick rode up to the top, he reached over and flipped his board!

The board twirled around and landed on the flat table at the top of the half-pipe.

Yeah!

Ollie fingerflip!

Nick landed on the board as the timer buzzed.

No falls that time, thought Nick, and then he heard the crowd cheering.

Nick rode his board down and off the pipe.

There was Mom! She came up to Nick and hugged him.

"That was great, Nick!" she said. "It looked just like your skateboard videos."

"Thanks, Mom," said Nick.

Josh came over and they slapped their hands in the air for a high five.

A big guy with dark glasses came over to Nick. "I'd like to talk with you."

"Uh, sure," said Nick.

"I'm Ben," said the guy.

"I own the bike shop on Second and Main. I really liked your moves on the half pipe."

"Thanks," said Nick.

"I'd like to sponsor you," said Ben, "so we can let people know that we're selling boards at our store now."

"A sponsor?" said Mom.

"Yes, ma'am," said Ben. "We'd take Nick here all over the county and have him ride for us."

"How would you like that, Nick?" asked Mom. "It means not being top grom, though."

Nick smiled. "I'd like that a lot!"

"Hey, Nick," said Josh. "Look at the scores!"

Nick looked up at the board.

1 – Nick Jackson

2 – Josh Abernathy

3 – Brandon Dorian

Yeah! First place!

About the Author

Anastasia Suen is the author of more than seventy books for young people. She made her first skateboard from a board and an old skate! Anastasia grew up in Florida and now lives with her family in Plano, Texas.

About the Illustrator

When Sean Tiffany was growing up, he lived on a small island off the coast of Maine. Every day, from sixth grade until he graduated from high school, he had to take a boat to get to school. When Sean isn't working on his art, he works on a multimedia project called "OilCan Drive," which combines music and art. He has a pet cactus named Jim.

Glossary

air (AIR)—riding with all four wheels off the ground

backside (BAK-side)—when a trick is done with the rider's back turned toward the ramp or obstacle

grind (GRYND)—scraping one or both axles on a rail, curb, or other surface

half-pipe (HAF PIPE)—a U-shaped ramp with a flat section in the middle

ledge (LEJ)—the top edge of a half-pipe ramp

ollie (OLL-lee)—a basic skateboard jump performed by tapping the tail on the ground

street skating (STREET SKAYT-ing)—skating on street, curbs, benches, handrails, and other city street items

vert ramp (VURT ramp)—a half-pipe, usually with ramps that are eight feet tall and almost vertical

vert skating (VURT SKAYT-ing)—skating on ramps and other vertical structures built for skating

Taking Care of Your Skateboard

Skateboards, just like any other piece of equipment, need to be maintained. They should be kept out of wet weather and their parts need to be checked regularly. Otherwise, instead of doing an ollie, you might end up upside down on the ground!

The first thing to do is make a maintenance checklist. Put it up wherever you store your skateboard. Mark the date on the checklist every time you work on your board. You should try to do it once a week. If you need extra tools, your local skate shop can help you figure out what to buy.

A list of what you should check is on the next page. If you want, you can add other things to the list. For example, once a week you could add a new sticker, or try a new trick!

Skateboard Maintenance Checklist

1 Wheels
Skateboard wheels wear down after a while and need to be replaced. Check your wheels for wear, and if they look worn, buy a replacement set. The skate shop can help you learn how to replace the wheels yourself. If a wheel is only worn on one edge, you can take it off, turn it around, and replace it.

2 Bearings (metal balls inside the wheels)
Bearings help your wheels move smoothly. They get squeaky and rusted sometimes, especially if your board has gotten wet. They should be cleaned with a lubricant, like oil, and greased.

3 Deck (the flat part of the skateboard that you stand on)
Make sure that there are no chips or cracks on the deck. If there's a small chip, and it's still attached, you can fix it with a little glue. But if there's a major chip, you will need to replace your board.

4 Trucks (trucks connect the wheels to the board)
If your trucks are loose, your wheels will wobble. Test them often, and tighten them with a screwdriver.

Discussion Questions

1. The main character, Nick, doesn't want to wear his wrist guards. If you were his friend, what would you tell him to change his mind?

2. Do you think it was fair that Nick's mother grounded him? Why or why not?

3. Why did the bike shop guy want to sponsor Nick?

Writing Prompts

1. What do you think was going through Nick's mind as he waited for the X-ray results? How would you feel if you were waiting? Describe your feelings.

2. How do you prepare yourself to play your favorite sport?

3. If you could ride the half-pipe like Nick, what moves would you try? Describe what you see and hear and feel as you are doing your moves.

Internet Sites

Do you want to know more about subjects related to this book? Or are you interested in learning about other topics? Then check out FactHound, a fun, easy way to find Internet sites.

Our investigative staff has already sniffed out great sites for you!

Here's how to use FactHound:

1. Visit *www.facthound.com*

2. Select your grade level.

3. To learn more about subjects related to this book, type in the book's ISBN number: **1598890646**.

4. Click the **Fetch It** button.

FactHound will fetch the best Internet sites for you!